DISNEY's
Frankenpooh

Bruce Talkington   Illustrated by John Kurtz

DISNEY PRESS

New York

Based on the Pooh storied by A. A. Milne (copyright The Pooh Properties Trust).
Printed and bound in the United States of America.

First small-format edition.
1 3 5 7 9 10 8 6 4 2

Library of Congress Catalog Card Number: 97-81144
ISBN: 0-7868-3177-4

For more Disney Press fun, visit www.DisneyBooks.com

DISNEY'S

Frankenpooh

It was the sort of crisp and sparkling autumn afternoon in the Hundred-Acre Wood that filled the heart of a very small animal with a story bursting to be told and desperate to be listened to.

And, at Piglet's house, where he had just finished hosting a small tea for his friends Rabbit, Pooh, Tigger, and Gopher, Piglet announced quietly that telling a story was just what he was going to do!

Tigger leaped out of the overstuffed armchair he was sharing with Rabbit and Gopher to where Piglet was standing nervously on the hearth.

"Is it a ghost story full o' spookables an' horribibble creatures an' things that go shoppin' in the night? Or," Tigger gasped as he clutched himself in a delightful tingle of terror, "is it about a MAD–scientist type?"

"Oh, no!" protested Piglet. "Not mad at all! Quite happy and cheerful, really." Then, clearing his throat carefullly, he began the story. "Once upon a time . . ."

Tigger listened for a moment then interrupted. "Say, it's the broad daylight! Even a not-so-scary story has to happen at night, ya know!"

The picture in Piglet's head of a beautiful castle on a bright summer's day suddenly grew very dark. "Oh, dear," he murmured to himself.

"An'," continued Tigger, "a nice thunderstorm wouldn't hurt either!"

Piglet's ears drooped as his imagination included a fierce thunderstorm crashing and rattling around the castle in his story.

But Piglet wasn't ready to give up. He had a story to tell and he was going to tell it his way, if no one minded very much.

Piglet thought about what glorious snacks he could whip up in a spotlessly neat and busily buzzing laboratory if he were a pleasant and very cheerful scientist. He wasn't a bit mad. He wasn't even slightly annoyed. Not even at Tigger.

"Mmm," Piglet said as he imagined the scientist holding a dripping sandwich. "Peanut butter and jelly. My favorite. And so very good for you, too!"

"Gasp!" Tigger suddenly interrupted Piglet's thoughts.

"What is it?" Piglet demanded. "What is it?"

"If you're gonna tell a story about a scientist," Tigger's voice continued, "he ought to at least be doin' somethin' terribibble, like creatin' a boogly, boogly MONSTER!"

"A monster?" Piglet answered in a tiny, not-very-hopeful-that-the-story-was-going-to-go-his-way sort of voice.

"Yeah!" responded the irrepressible Tigger. "The monster . . . FRANKENPOOH!"

The scientist looked at Frankenpooh with mixed feelings. Pooh? A MONSTER?

"Yeah!" Tigger continued. "That's absitutely perfect. Only he oughta be bigger than that!"

And at once Frankenpooh grew bigger! And bigger and bigger until the very small scientist felt very small indeed!

"Oh, bother," sighed Frankenpooh as he bumped his head on the top of the page.

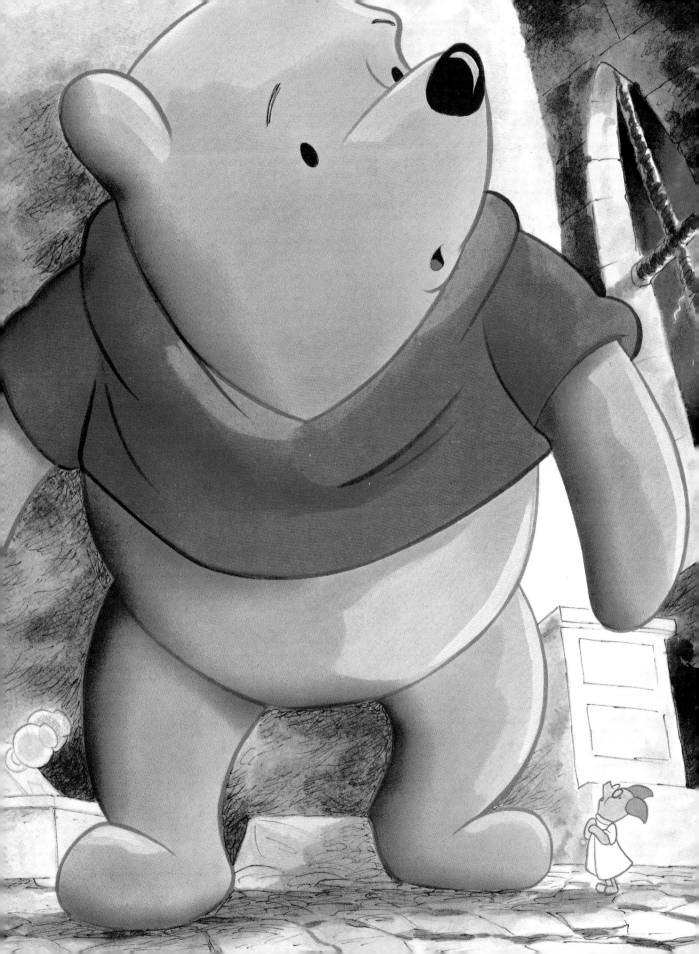

"Now that's what I call a monster," hooted Tigger. "Hoo-hoo-hoo!"

The very small scientist ran around the monster's feet in a frightened flurry of activity, shouting, "Oh, help me! Oh, save me!"

"This is very terrifryin'," Tigger chuckled, delighted.

The monster Frankenpooh, after much think-think-thinking and scratching of oversized ears, reached a monstrous conclusion.

"I want . . . honey?" he announced in a voice so loud he surprised himself.

And he went looking for a not-so-small smackeral of something sweet to eat.

"Honey!" he announced again just because he liked the sound of it.

"And the monster Frankenpooh," announced Tigger, "went lookin' high and low for whatever it is monster Frankenpoohs look for."

"Honey," boomed Frankenpooh as if to remind him.

"An' the villagers skidaddled for life and lumber," continued Tigger. "Trembling in your socks, aren't ya? Clinging to the edge of your seats? But there's no stoppin' the gigantical monstrous monstrosity!"

"An' everybody was up to their necks in arms," added Tigger dramatically, "because they knew who it was that was responsibibble for the horribibblest monster that was terror-fryin' them."

"Oh, d-d-dear," moaned the scientist as he found himself surrounded by the full-of-wrath villagers.

"Help!" squeaked the scientist. "Stop the story! Please! It was an accident! I didn't mean to do it! I just wanted it to be a nice, not-so-scary story."

And Piglet opened his eyes to discover himself back on the hearth of his very own fireplace surrounded by his good friends Tigger, Rabbit, and Gopher.

"But, Piglet," soothed Tigger, "it was nothin' to get so upset about."

"It was just a s-s-silly s-s-story," whistled Gopher.

"Of course, Piglet," added Rabbit gently. "There was no monster. And no one's angry at you."

Piglet looked around in great relief. "No?" he asked in a very small voice.

"No," his friends all assured him in one voice.

After his friends had settled Piglet in his favorite armchair and given him a cup of his favorite hot chocolate, Rabbit put his arm comfortingly around Piglet's very small shoulder.

"You really should learn the difference between what's real and what isn't," Rabbit told him gently. "Shouldn't he, POOH?"

"Yes, Piglet," responded the very large and Frankenpooh-looking bear, "you really should. And so should I."

Then he emitted quite the largest Pooh Bear sort of sigh they had ever heard. "Oh, bother."

And Pooh did eventually get the story straightened out in his head full of fluff, and returned to the convenient size proper to the amounts of honey required to feed an always hungry bear.